This book
belongs to:

Or would you go to the **city**, be frien
fountain in it, travel by **rickshaw**, eat
and a **deer-stalker hat**, keep a pet **tou**
for fun and sleep in a **bunk bed**? Or w
ghost, live in a **wigwam** with a **trampol**
and **mash**, wear a **denim jacket** with a
fashion model, blow **bubbles** and
the **seaside**, be friends with a **Viking**,
in it, travel by **limousine**, eat a box of c
hat and **fluffy mules**, keep a pet **eleph**
and sleep in a **kennel**? Or would you go
a **tower block** with a **secret door** in it,
a **poncho** with **stilettos** and a **furry**
line-dancing and sleep on a **camp-bed**?
be friends with an **alien**, live in a **li**
canoe, eat a bag of **crisps**, wear a **kilt**
a pet **unicorn**, be an **astronaut**,

ith a **pirate**, live in a **spaceship** with a

er, wear a **suit of armour** with **trainers**

be a **deep-sea diver**, build a **snowman**

you go to the **moon**, be friends with a

n it, travel by **paddle boat**, eat **sausages**

a and **wedges**, keep a pet **monkey**, be a

in a **shoe**? Or would you go to

n a **fairy palace** with a **ping-pong table**

olates, wear a **grass skirt** with a **cowboy**

be a **hairdresser**, go on a **bouncy castle**

a **desert**, be friends with a **knight**, live in

el by **helicopter**, eat a **hamburger**, wear

keep a pet **spider**, be a **magician**, go

would you go to the top of a **mountain**,

ouse with **chandeliers** in it, travel by

h **winkle-pickers** and a **sombrero**, keep

jigsaw and sleep in a **hammock**?

In memory of Henry Brown
N.S.

To everyone at Browsers Bookshop
P.G.

PICTURE CORGI

UK | USA | Canada | Ireland | Australia
India | New Zealand | South Africa

Picture Corgi is part of the Penguin Random House group of companies
whose addresses can be found at global.penguinrandomhouse.com.

www.penguin.co.uk   www.puffin.co.uk   www.ladybird.co.uk

Penguin
Random House
UK

First published 2003
This edition published 2017

001

A CIP catalogue record for this book is available from the British Library
Printed in China
ISBN: 978-0-552-57706-9

All correspondence to:
Picture Corgi, Penguin Random House Children's
80 Strand, London WC2R 0RL

FSC
www.fsc.org
MIX
Paper from
responsible sources
FSC® C018179

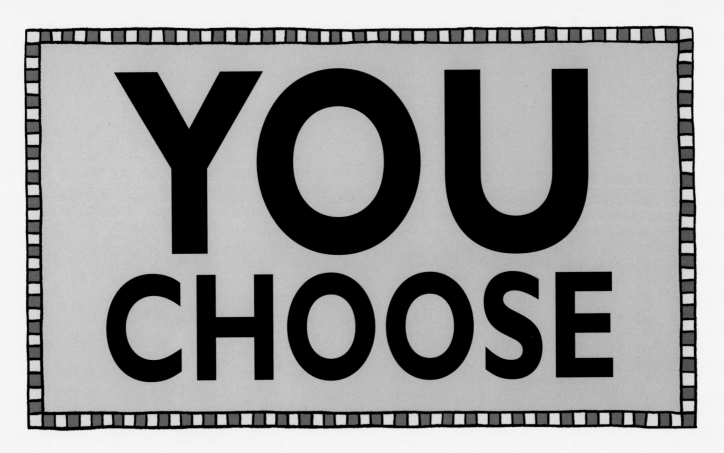

YOU CHOOSE

Imagine you could have anything you wanted!

What sort of things do you mean?

Just turn the pages of this book, have a look and choose.

Words by Pippa Goodhart, pictures by Nick Sharratt

Picture Corgi

If you could go anywhere,

where would you go?

I want her to be my friend.

family and friends?

What kind of home

would you choose?

And what would you put in it?

Would you travel with wheels or wings?

Or perhaps choose one of these other things?

When you got hungry,

what would you eat?

Choose some shoes ...

...and perhaps a hat?

Why not get yourself a pet...

Is there a job

What would you do...

...for fun?

And when you got tired and felt like a snooze,

where would you sleep? You choose. Goodnight!

Or would you go to the desert, be f
caravan with a **drum set** in it, travel by
with **flip-flops** and a **furry hat**, keep a
for fun and sleep in a **cradle**? Or would
live in a **cave** with a **swimming pool** i
wear a **tuxedo** with **Roman sandals** and
go on a **roller coaster** and sleep in
outer space, be friends with a **baby**,
on it, travel by **steam train**, eat a **waterm**
lacy boots, keep a pet **polar bear**, b
sleep in a **hammock**? Or would you g
live in a **cottage** with a **secret door** in i
wear a **kilt** with **clogs** and a top
bird watching and sleep on a **nest**? C
be friends with a **vampire**, live in a tr
by **space shuttle**, eat **squid**, wear a bo
keep a pet **bat**, be a **deep-sea diver**

ds with Superwoman, live in a gypsy
hip, eat sponge cake, wear a feather boa
dragon, be a clown, make phone calls
go to the seaside, be friends with a wolf,
travel by helicopter, drink milkshakes,
nnet, keep a pet lizard, be an astronaut,
bed of flowers? Or would you go to
e on a toadstool with a glitter light
n, wear dungarees with a sailor's hat and
n architect, go bungee jumping and
the moon, be friends with a gangster,
avel by paraglider, eat corn-on-the-cob,
keep a pet panda, be a pilot, go
ould you go to the top of a waterfall,
ouse with a rocking horse in it, travel
e with ballet shoes and a panama hat,
d a book and sleep in a space-bed?

Why not
choose some more books
illustrated by Nick Sharratt